Praise for *The Librarian of Auschwitz* novel

★ "An unforgettable, heartbreaking novel."
—*Publishers Weekly*, starred review

★ "Like Markus Zusak's *The Book Thief*, it's a sophisticated novel with mature themes, delivering an emotionally searing reading experience. An important novel that will stand with other powerful testaments from the Holocaust era."
—*Booklist*, starred review

★ "This novel is one that could easily be recommended or taught alongside Elie Wiesel's *Night* and *The Diary of Anne Frank* and a text that, once read, will never be forgotten. A hauntingly authentic Holocaust retelling; a must for YA collections."
—*School Library Journal*, starred review

★ "Though no punches are pulled about the unimaginable atrocity of the death camps, a life-affirming history."
—*Kirkus Reviews*, starred review

★ "*The Librarian of Auschwitz* is a heartbreaking and ultimately inspiring work of art."
—*Shelf Awareness*, starred review

★ "Iturbe's remarkable account uses an immediate present tense to immerse readers in Dita's story as she goes about what constitutes daily life in Auschwitz, all the while risking everything to distribute and hide the library's books."
—*The Horn Book*, starred review

THE LIBRARIAN OF AUSCHWITZ

HENRY HOLT AND COMPANY, *PUBLISHERS SINCE 1866*
HENRY HOLT® IS A REGISTERED TRADEMARK OF MACMILLAN PUBLISHING GROUP, LLC
120 BROADWAY, NEW YORK, NY 10271 • MACKIDS.COM

OUR BOOKS MAY BE PURCHASED IN BULK FOR PROMOTIONAL, EDUCATIONAL, OR BUSINESS USE. PLEASE CONTACT YOUR LOCAL BOOKSELLER OR THE MACMILLAN CORPORATE AND PREMIUM SALES DEPARTMENT AT (800) 221-7945 EXT. 5442 OR BY EMAIL AT MACMILLANSPECIALMARKETS@MACMILLAN.COM.

LIBRARY OF CONGRESS CATALOGING-IN-PUBLICATION DATA IS AVAILABLE.

FIRST PUBLISHED IN SPAIN BY EDITORIAL PLANETA IN 2022
FIRST AMERICAN EDITION, 2023
BOOK DESIGN BY LISA VEGA
PRINTED IN CHINA BY 1010 PRINTING INTERNATIONAL LIMITED, KWUN TONG, HONG KONG

ISBN 978-1-250-84299-2 (HARDCOVER)
1 3 5 7 9 10 8 6 4 2

ISBN 978-1-250-84298-5 (PAPERBACK)
1 3 5 7 9 10 8 6 4 2

Война
и
мир

THE LIBRARIAN OF AUSCHWITZ

BASED ON THE NOVEL BY ANTONIO ITURBE

ADAPTED BY SALVA RUBIO

TRANSLATED BY LILIT ŽEKULIN THWAITES

ILLUSTRATED BY LORETO AROCA

GODWIN BOOKS

HENRY HOLT AND COMPANY

NEW YORK

BACK THEN, SHE WAS JUST A CHILD...

A WINDOW INTO HERSELF AND ONTO THE WORLD.

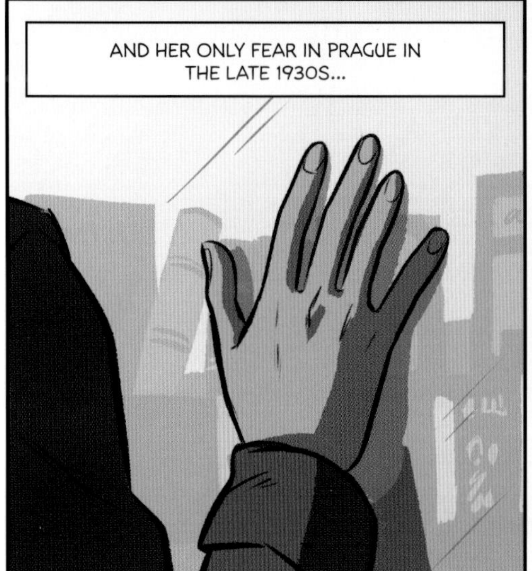
AND HER ONLY FEAR IN PRAGUE IN THE LATE 1930S...

HP LOVECRAFT
...WAS THAT SHE WOULDN'T HAVE ENOUGH TIME TO READ EVERYTHING SHE WANTED TO.

HER NAME WAS EDITA ADLEROVÁ,
BUT EVERYONE CALLED HER DITA...

...AND BOOKS WERE HER LIFE.

DITA, I'VE FINISHED. LET'S GO HOME!

HAVE YOU ALREADY DECIDED WHICH BOOK YOU'RE CHOOSING?
HMM... YES...NO... JUST A MINUTE!

YOU'VE SPENT 30 MINUTES DECIDING! WE HAVEN'T GOT ALL DAY.
YES, FINE... IT'S... IT'S... I WANT THEM ALL!

WHY DO YOU WANT THEM ALL?
YOU'VE GOT ALL THE TIME IN THE WORLD TO READ THEM ONE BY ONE.

IT'S JUST... I DON'T KNOW!
THEN DECIDE TOMORROW.

CAN I BUY TWO TOMORROW?
FINE! FINE! BUT ONLY IF YOU FINISH THE ONE YOU'RE READING NOW.

PAPA!

MY LITTLE LITERARY CRITIC. HOW MANY BOOKS HAVE YOU BOUGHT TODAY?
MAMA SAYS I HAVE TO FINISH THE ONE I'M READING FIRST.
OKAY, OKAY! BUT IF YOU CONTINUE AT THIS RATE, YOUR BOOKS WON'T FIT IN OUR HOUSE!

COME ON. LET'S SEE WHAT WE'LL DO IN OUR GEOGRAPHY LESSON TODAY.
LET'S SPIN, AND...

HIMA... HIMALAYA!
MY GOODNESS! YOU'VE LANDED ON THE HIGHEST MOUNTAIN RANGE IN THE WORLD!

THE ADLERS WERE AN ORDINARY CZECH FAMILY...
...BUT THESE WEREN'T ORDINARY TIMES.

IT WAS A TIME WHEN EVERY CHILD
DESERVED A NORMAL CHILDHOOD...

...A TIME TO DREAM,
IMAGINE, LAUGH...

...A TIME OF DISCOVERY AND
ENJOYMENT.

?
BUT IT WAS A DIFFERENT
STORY FOR ADULTS.

FOR THEM, IT WAS A TIME OF ANXIETY AND UNEASE...

...A PERIOD OF DARKNESS, FULL OF FEAR.

THOUSANDS OF CHILDHOODS...
...THOUSANDS OF FANTASIES...

...THOUSANDS OF DREAMS...
BRRR
BRRR

...ABOUT TO BE DESTROYED.
BRRRRR
BRRRR

BRRRR
BRRRR

BRRRR

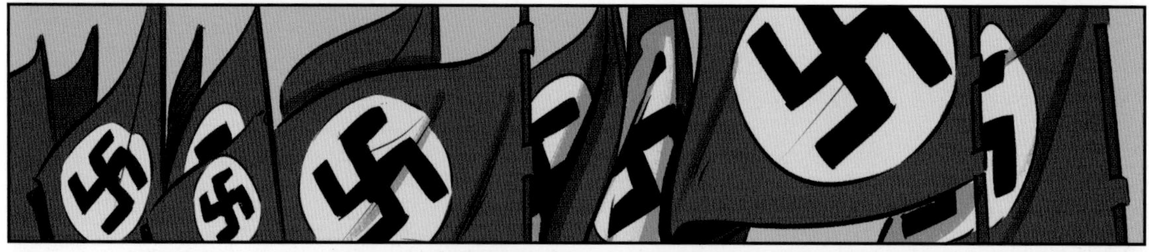

THAT WAS THE DAY DITA LEFT HER CHILDHOOD BEHIND...
...BECAUSE THAT WAS THE DAY SHE STARTED TO FEAR MEN.

THE NAZIS HAD ARRIVED
IN CZECHOSLOVAKIA

THEY HATED THE JEWS; NOBODY KNEW
WHAT WAS GOING TO HAPPEN TO THEM.

THE JEWS COULD ONLY PRETEND THAT
THINGS WERE STILL NORMAL

BUT EVEN A CHILD COULD SEE THAT NOTHING
WAS EVER GOING TO BE THE SAME AGAIN.

ONE DAY, DITA WAS WALKING
PAST THE CAFÉ CONTINENTAL.

SHE NOW UNDERSTOOD THE MANY WHISPERED
CONVERSATIONS BETWEEN HER PARENTS.

HER FATHER HAD BEEN FIRED SOME TIME AGO...

...BUT HER PARENTS DIDN'T WANT DITA TO KNOW.

PAPA... THE SCHOOL HAS GIVEN US...

..."HOLIDAYS."

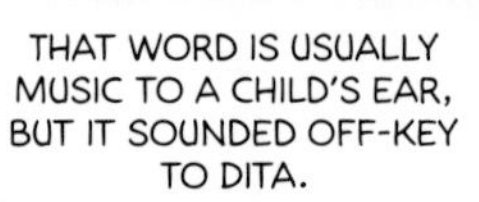
THAT WORD IS USUALLY MUSIC TO A CHILD'S EAR, BUT IT SOUNDED OFF-KEY TO DITA.

DON'T WORRY. YOU CAN STUDY AT HOME.
WE STILL HAVE OUR BOOKS.

BUT WHAT COULD BOOKS DO?

WHAT COULD BOOKS DO IN THE FACE OF WHAT WAS ABOUT TO LAND ON THEM?

DITA, LISTEN...
WE HAVE TO TALK TO YOU.

WE HAVE TO MOVE, DITA.

WHAT? I'M NOT LEAVING THIS PLACE!

THIS IS NOT THE MOMENT TO COMPLAIN!
WHACK!!

BUT MAMA... WHY DO WE HAVE TO...?

FORGIVE ME, DITA.
IT'S... IT'S THE WAR.

THINGS ARE CHANGING VERY QUICKLY.

WE WON'T BE ABLE TO GO OUTDOORS NOW WITHOUT THIS YELLOW STAR.

WE JEWS MUST ALWAYS WEAR ONE.

BANS WERE IMPOSED ON ALL JEWS. NO ENTRY INTO CAFÉS AND NO SHOPPING AT THE SAME TIME AS NON-JEWS; NO ACCESS TO MOVIES; NO RADIOS... EVEN BUYING APPLES WAS FORBIDDEN.

CHILDREN WEREN'T EVEN PERMITTED TO PLAY IN PARKS... BUT THERE WAS STILL THE JEWISH CEMETERY.
FOLLOW ME! IT'S THIS WAY...
ARE YOU SURE, DITA?
THIS PLACE SCARES ME!
YOU'RE GOING TO GET US INTO TROUBLE...

HERE YOU HAVE HIM— THE CREATOR OF THE GOLEM.

LEGEND HAS IT...

...THAT A RABBI DECIPHERED THE WORD WITH WHICH YAHWEH INSTILLED THE GIFT OF LIFE. AND AN UNCONTROLLABLE COLOSSUS WAS CREATED...

...AND WHEN THE JEWISH PEOPLE FIND THEMSELVES IN DANGER, THE GOLEM WILL RETURN TO SAVE US.

WHAT RUBBISH!
SUCH LEGENDS ARE LIES.
THAT'S A STORY FOR KIDS.
DITA BELIEVES EVERYTHING SHE READS IN BOOKS.

YOU'LL SEE. HE'LL COME.

ONE AFTERNOON, A SUMMONS FINALLY ARRIVED FROM THE JEWISH COUNCIL OF PRAGUE.

IS IT TRUE? DO WE HAVE TO LEAVE PRAGUE?

YES, DARLING. WE HAVE TO GO TO TEREZÍN.

WE CAN ONLY TAKE 50 KILOS EACH, RIGHT?
YES. I'LL GO AND SEE HOW DITA'S DOING.

DITA, HAVE YOU FINISHED? ...OH!

ARE YOU ALL RIGHT, DARLING?

I WANT TO TAKE ALL MY BOOKS.

DITA, WE CAN ONLY TAKE ONE SUITCASE EACH.
BOOKS WEIGH TOO MUCH. YOU'RE GOING TO NEED CLOTHES...OTHER THINGS.

WHAT AM I GOING TO DO WITHOUT MY BOOKS? WHAT'S GOING TO HAPPEN TO THEM?

WELL, PERHAPS... MAYBE YOU'LL FIND OTHER BOOKS, DARLING.
BUT NOW IS NOT THE TIME TO BE THINKING ABOUT THIS.

NOT LONG AFTER THIS, MANY JEWS, INCLUDING THE ADLERS, WERE ORDERED TO REPORT TO THE BUBNY TRAIN STATION. FROM THERE, THEY WERE TAKEN TO THE TEREZÍN GHETTO, AND SOME TIME LATER, THEY WERE AGAIN PUT ON A TRAIN TO AUSCHWITZ.

THEY THOUGHT THEY WERE GOING TO TRAVEL LIKE ORDINARY PEOPLE...

...BUT THE NAZIS MADE IT PERFECTLY CLEAR WHAT THEY THOUGHT OF THEM.

THEY WERE INFERIOR BEINGS...

...AND THEIR LIVES WERE WORTHLESS.

ARBEIT MACHT FREI

AUSCHWITZ...

WHAT WAS GOING TO HAPPEN TO THEM NOW?

?

NO ONE KNEW...

...BUT THINGS DIDN'T SEEM VERY HOPEFUL.

THEY COULD ONLY BE BRAVE...

...COMMEND THEMSELVES TO GOD, AND LIVE OR DIE.

THEY THOUGHT THEY WERE GOING TO BE GASSED RIGHT THERE. BUT STRANGE AS IT MAY SEEM, ONLY WATER CAME OUT OF THE SHOWER HEADS... FREEZING COLD, BUT WATER.
WHY WEREN'T THEY DEAD ALREADY?

THE DISINFECTION PROCESS WAS JUST AS PAINFUL.

BUT THEY WERE STILL ALIVE.

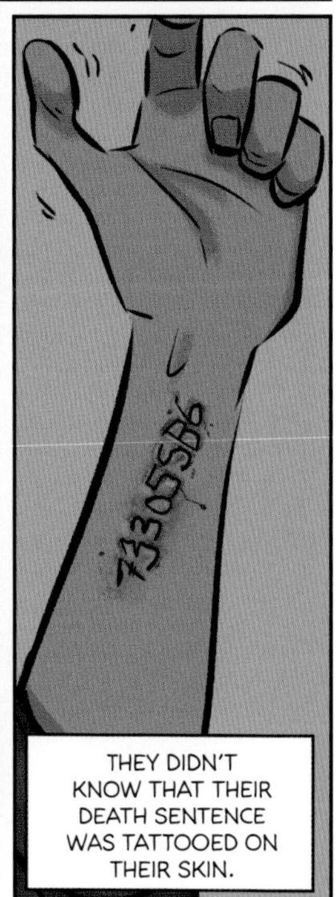
73305586
THEY DIDN'T KNOW THAT THEIR DEATH SENTENCE WAS TATTOOED ON THEIR SKIN.

BUT THERE WERE MORE SURPRISES IN STORE FOR THEM.

NO ONE'S HEAD WAS SHAVED; EVERYONE KEPT THEIR OWN CLOTHES.
BUT WHAT WAS MOST INCREDIBLE...

...FAMILIES WERE ALLOWED TO STAY TOGETHER.

NO ONE KNEW WHY...BUT FOR THE TIME BEING THEY WERE GOING TO BE TOGETHER, AND NOTHING ELSE MATTERED.

RECENT ARRIVALS, LISTEN TO ME!

MEN AND WOMEN MUST SLEEP IN DIFFERENT BARRACKS.
FIND YOURSELVES A BUNK; YOU'LL HAVE TO SHARE.

CHILDREN UNDER FOURTEEN ARE EXEMPT FROM WORK.
THEY'LL SPEND THE DAY IN OUR CHILDREN'S HUT.
WHO WAS THIS MAN?

HE WAS JEWISH LIKE THE REST OF THEM...
...SO WHY WAS HE SPEAKING WITH SUCH AUTHORITY?

PROFESSOR MORGENSTERN WILL BRING YOU UP TO DATE ON EVERYTHING ELSE.

DON'T BE AFRAID OF FREDY. HA HA!
HE MIGHT SEEM A BIT STRICT, BUT HE'S A GOOD MAN.

MEN AND WOMEN WERE SEPARATED

AND EACH PERSON HAD TO FIND THEIR OWN BUNK.

UP TO THREE PEOPLE SLEPT IN A SINGLE BUNK.
THERE WERE FIGHTS FOR EACH SHEET OR BLANKET.

LEAVE IT, DITA... WE'LL FIND A PLACE TO–
WAIT, MAMA. I KNOW WHAT I'M DOING.

DITA, WHERE ARE YOU GOING?

HEY! WHERE DO YOU THINK YOU'RE GOING, KIDDO?
LISTEN, YOU!
WHAT? HOW DARE YOU SPEAK TO ME LIKE THAT?

TWENTY OR THIRTY MORE WOMEN ARE GOING TO COME LOOKING FOR A SPOT.
SOME OF THEM ARE FAT, OTHERS ARE SICK, AND YOU WOULDN'T BE COMFORTABLE.

MY MOTHER AND I ARE SMALL AND SKINNY...
...WE DON'T SNORE, AND WE WASH EVERY DAY.
WHERE DO YOU THINK YOU'RE GOING TO FIND BETTER BEDMATES?

FINE. YOU'RE STAYING WITH ME.
MAMA, CLIMB UP!

THAT NIGHT, DITA UNDERSTOOD THAT SHE'D HAVE TO BE BRAVE TO SURVIVE...
...BUT SHE ALSO LEARNED THAT SURVIVAL WAS POSSIBLE.

WAKE UP, WAKE UP! YOU DISGUSTING CREATURES.
WHACK
THE KAPOS WOKE THEM UP EACH DAY AT 5:30 AM.
THEY HAD TO BE QUICK OR THE KAPO WOULD HIT THEM.
WHACK
WHACK

THEY DID THE ROLL CALL EVERY DAY.
IF THEY DIDN'T LISTEN CAREFULLY FOR THEIR NUMBER, THE KAPOS HIT THEM AGAIN.

AS SHE GOT USED TO HER NEW SITUATION,
DITA COULDN'T HELP BUT WONDER:

WHY ARE WE DIFFERENT IN OUR CAMP BIIB??

WHY CAN WE KEEP OUR OWN CLOTHES AND OUR HAIR?
WHY ARE OUR FAMILIES STILL TOGETHER?

WHY?

YOU'RE DITA, AREN'T YOU? I'M PROFESSOR MORGENSTERN.
COME, I'LL INTRODUCE YOU TO SOME FRIENDS.

THIS IS MARGIT, ONE OF OUR BEST WORKERS.
I'M DITA.

AND THIS IS OTA. HE'S A BIT OF A KNOW-IT-ALL, BUT A GOOD LAD.
HI, OTA.
H-HI, DITA.

MOST IMPORTANT, DON'T GO NEAR THE *KAPOS*.
I WOULDN'T DARE. THEY'RE SCARY.

THEY'LL GIVE YOU A BEATING FOR WHATEVER REASON.

AND ALSO, BE CAREFUL OF...
GOOD MORNING, ALL. ARE THEY READY, PROFESSOR?

AH, GOOD MORNING, FREDY.
DITA COULDN'T HELP FEELING SOMEWHAT INTIMIDATED.

THE MAN CALLED FREDY HAD A REMARKABLE PRESENCE.
DIGNIFIED, ELEGANT, POWERFUL.
DITA COULDN'T AVOID THINKING OF...THE GOLEM.

WE'RE LUCKY WE CAN COUNT ON YOU, PROFESSOR. YOU'RE SO MUCH HELP.
ANYONE WOULD DO THE SAME THING, FREDY.

WELCOME. WE NEED YOUR HELP TO MAKE THE FAMILY CAMP, BIIB, A BETTER PLACE.
WHAT WERE YOU DOING BEFORE YOU ARRIVED HERE?

I WAS A TEACHER.
GREAT! WE NEED PEOPLE LIKE YOU.

THANK YOU. WE'RE ALL A BIT SCARED.
I GET IT. IT'S A COMPLICATED PLACE.

I'M DITA. I LIKE TO READ.
IT'S NOT MUCH, BUT I'LL HELP HOWEVER I CAN.

DELIGHTED, DITA. READING IS VERY IMPORTANT.
I'M SURE WE'LL FIND A PLACE FOR YOU.
ER... THANK YOU.

WHO WAS THIS MAN?

IN GERMANY, AFTER THE DEATH OF HIS FATHER, FREDY HIRSCH FOUND A HOME IN YOUTH GROUPS.
HE JOINED THE JPD, A GERMAN JEWISH SCOUT GROUP. AT THE AGE OF FIFTEEN, HE WAS ALREADY GIVING TALKS AND HE WAS A FERVENT ZIONIST.
FACED WITH GROWING ANTISEMITISM, THE ORGANIZATION BECAME MILITANT, AND FREDY DISCOVERED THE BENEFITS OF PHYSICAL TRAINING.
HE BECAME AN ATHLETE AND HELPED ORGANIZE THE MACCABI GAMES IN PRAGUE, ATTENDED BY THOUSANDS.
BUT AFTER HE WAS ARRESTED FOR SUBVERSIVE ACTIVITIES IN TEREZÍN, HE WAS TRANSPORTED TO AUSCHWITZ, ALONG WITH SO MANY OTHERS.

WHEN HE ARRIVED AT AUSCHWITZ, HE WASN'T INTIMIDATED. INSTEAD, HE BEHAVED LIKE A LEADER AND OBTAINED VARIOUS PRIVILEGES FOR OTHER PRISONERS.

A BLOCK, FOR EXAMPLE, WHERE THE CHILDREN COULD BE LOOKED AFTER WHILE THEIR PARENTS WORKED...AND HE BECAME ITS SUPERVISOR.

PERHAPS BECAUSE OF HIS DIGNIFIED BEARING AND ATTENTION TO APPEARANCE, THE GERMANS AND *KAPOS* RESPECTED HIM.

HE WAS AFRAID OF NOTHING AND INSTILLED CONFIDENCE AMONG THE OTHER PRISONERS.
BUT NOBODY REALLY SEEMED TO KNOW HIM.

MEANWHILE, DITA AND HER PARENTS WERE GETTING TO KNOW THE CAMP.
SO... DO YOU ALL HAVE YOUR JOBS YET?
WELL, MARGIT, YES, MY PARENTS DO.

AUSCHWITZ WAS ALSO A LABOR CAMP, AND THE INHABITANTS OF CAMP BIIB SPENT MOST OF THE DAY WORKING.
MY FATHER HAS TO MAKE GUN BELTS FOR THE GERMAN ARMY.
AND MY MOTHER HAS TO MAKE CAPS FOR THE SOLDIERS.

IT'S HARD PHYSICAL WORK, AND THEY'RE NOT USED TO IT.

WELL, THEY'VE BEEN PRETTY LUCKY.
AT LEAST THEY'RE INDOORS. THERE ARE JOBS THAT ARE WORSE.
I KNOW...

THERE ARE PEOPLE WHO DIG OUT THE DITCHES...

THE WORK DETAIL THAT HAULS LOADS OF BUILDING MATERIAL ALL DAY...

THE PEOPLE CHARGED WITH EMPTYING THE LATRINES...

AND WHAT'S UNDOUBTEDLY THE WORST JOB, THOSE WHO COLLECT THE CORPSES.

IN A NUTSHELL, DITA...WE HAVE TO FIND YOU A GOOD JOB OR WHO KNOWS WHERE YOU'LL END UP.
YES, BUT WHO CAN...?

I'VE GOT IT! LET'S GO AND SEE MRS. TURNOVSKÁ.

OF COURSE WE HAVE TO FIND YOU A JOB!
HAVE YOU THOUGHT OF THE CHILDREN'S BLOCK?
WHAT'S THAT?

IT'S ONE OF THE PRIVILEGES FREDY GOT FOR US.
HE CONVINCED THE *KOMMANDANT* THAT A SEPARATE CHILDREN'S BLOCK WOULD BE THE BEST WAY TO KEEP THEM UNDER CONTROL.

SINCE YOU'RE FOURTEEN MAYBE YOU CAN BECOME AN ASSISTANT, AND HELP THE TEACHERS.
DITA, THAT'S PERFECT FOR YOU!

COME ON. WE'LL GO AND ASK MRS. EDELSTEIN.

I'VE SAID NO!
BUT MRS. EDELSTEIN, DITA–

...AND DITA IS VERY RESPONSIBLE.
SHE SPEAKS PERFECT CZECH AND GERMAN; SHE KNOWS HOW TO READ; SHE'S PATIENT AND–
I'VE SAID NO!
WE HAVE MORE THAN ENOUGH ASSISTANTS... EVERYONE WANTS THOSE POSITIONS.

WE'LL FIND YOU SOMETHING, DITA.
YES, DON'T WORRY. MAYBE IN–
WAIT A MINUTE...

DID YOU SAY YOU CAN READ GERMAN AND CZECH?

YES! PERFECTLY!
WELL THEN, MAYBE...

AND THAT WAS HOW DITA FIRST GOT INTO BLOCK 31.

INSTEAD OF CRAMMED BUNK BEDS, THERE WERE CHILDREN'S STOOLS.
INSTEAD OF DIRT, THE WALLS WERE COVERED WITH CHILDREN'S DRAWINGS.
INSTEAD OF SHOUTS AND THREATS, THERE WERE GAMES AND LAUGHTER.

YOU MUST BE DITA... OUR STAGE PROMPTER DIED YESTERDAY.
THEY TELL ME YOU CAN DO THE JOB WELL.
I'M SURE I CAN!

YOU'LL HAVE TO WHISPER THE LINES TO THE ACTORS WHO FORGET THEM.
LIKE LITTLE SARAH, WHO CAN'T SAY HER LINES IN GERMAN WHEN SHE GETS NERVOUS!
I UNDER-STAND...

BUT IT WASN'T ENOUGH TO READ THEM... DITA PRACTICALLY HAD TO MEMORIZE THE LINES IN ORDER TO DO HER JOB WELL.

THE DAY OF THE PERFORMANCE ARRIVED, AND DITA HAD TO WORK HARD.
THE ACTORS WERE ONLY AMATEURS AND THEIR NERVES MADE THEM FORGET THEIR LINES.

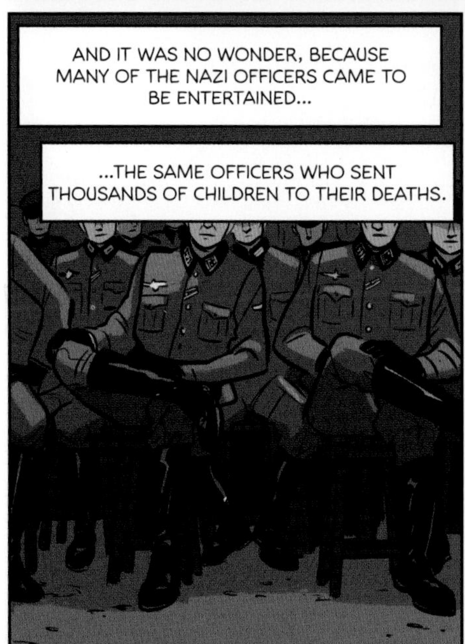
AND IT WAS NO WONDER, BECAUSE MANY OF THE NAZI OFFICERS CAME TO BE ENTERTAINED...
...THE SAME OFFICERS WHO SENT THOUSANDS OF CHILDREN TO THEIR DEATHS.

"YOU ARE THE FAIREST OF THEM ALL, MY QUEEN..."

DESPITE EVERYTHING, THE SHOW WAS A SUCCESS.
AND IT ACHIEVED THE IMPOSSIBLE: IT MADE PEOPLE FORGET FOR A FEW MINUTES THAT THEY WERE IN AUSCHWITZ.

THE PRISONERS WOULD LONG REMEMBER THOSE FEW MOMENTS OF HAPPINESS...

BUT THE NEXT DAY, DITA FOUND HERSELF WITHOUT A JOB AGAIN. ALTHOUGH...
DITA, MR. HIRSCH WANTS TO SEE YOU!

MR. HIRSCH? ME? BUT...
HURRY UP!

DID I DO SUCH A BAD JOB WITH THE PLAY THAT HE WANTS TO TELL ME OFF?

M-MR. HIRSCH... THEY SAID YOU WANTED TO SEE ME...
YOUR ARRIVAL IN THE CAMP IS TIMELY!
WHAT? BUT...

WE DESPERATELY NEED A LIBRARIAN!

ME? BUT I DON'T KNOW HOW...
I FINALLY REMEMBERED YOU. YOU WERE IN THE TEREZÍN GHETTO WHEN I WAS THERE.

DITA RECALLED THE TIME SHE'D SPENT IN TEREZÍN BEFORE ARRIVING IN AUSCHWITZ...
"I WAS IN CHARGE OF THE YOUTH OFFICE THERE."

"OUR JOB WAS TO ENSURE THAT THE YOUNG PEOPLE WERE CARING AND WORKED FOR THE BENEFIT OF ALL."

"AND THERE YOU WERE, SMALL AND SKINNY, BUT PUSHING THAT HEAVY TROLLEY OF BOOKS WITHOUT ANYONE ORDERING YOU TO DO IT."
THERE MUST BE SOME MISUNDERSTANDING. I WAS JUST HELPING TO DISTRIBUTE THE BOOKS. I'M NOT A LIBRARIAN.

"NO, DITA...YOU COULD HAVE BEEN WANDERING AROUND, LIKE SO MANY OTHERS...
"...BUT YOU WERE WORKING HARD, SO THAT OUR PEOPLE COULD READ."

SO, IF YOU ACCEPT, YOU WILL BE OUR LIBRARIAN.
O...KAY.

BUT I WARN YOU: IT WILL BE VERY DANGEROUS.
YOU COULD EVEN DIE.

BOOKS ARE BANNED. IF THE GUARDS CATCH YOU WITH A BOOK, THEY'LL EXECUTE YOU.
I UNDERSTAND.
YOU'RE NOT LISTENING TO ME, CHILD.

IT'S A HUGE RISK.
I DON'T MIND.
THEY COULD KILL YOU.
I REALLY DON'T CARE.

RUNNING OUR LIBRARY CALLS FOR A BRAVE PERSON...

THAT WAS WHEN DITA REALIZED THAT SHE WAS SHAKING ALL OVER.

S-SO YOU'RE NOT GOING TO COUNT ON ME?
DO YOU THINK I'M A SCAREDY-CAT?

ON THE CONTRARY. YOU STRIKE ME AS VERY COURAGEOUS.

BUT YOU CAN SEE THAT I'M SHAKING!

DITA, BRAVE PEOPLE ARE THOSE WHO CAN OVERCOME THEIR OWN FEAR. YOU ARE ONE OF THOSE.

WELL THEN, DITA, YOU ARE OUR NEW LIBRARIAN. AND PLEASE CALL ME FREDY.
TH-THANKS, FREDY.

WELL, DITA, THIS IS YOUR LIBRARY.

IT'S NOT MUCH.

JUST A HANDFUL OF BOOKS...

...AND SOME OF THEM AREN'T EVEN IN A LANGUAGE WE UNDERSTAND...

GEOMETRIE
H.G WELLS
Stručné
Dějiny
Světa
ATLAS
Světa
SIGMUND
FREUD
...BUT THEY ARE BOOKS.

AN ATLAS, A GEOMETRY BOOK, A HISTORY BOOK...A RUSSIAN GRAMMAR BOOK...

...A FRENCH NOVEL... A BOOK ON PSYCHOLOGY... ANOTHER NOVEL, THIS TIME IN RUSSIAN.
AH, AND THIS ONE IS IN A BAD STATE, AND NOT APPROPRIATE FOR CHILDREN, LET ALONE GIRLS.

WITH ALL DUE RESPECT, FREDY, AFTER SEEING THE POT WITH OUR BREAKFAST CROSS PATHS EVERY DAY WITH THE CART CARRYING THE DEAD...

...DO YOU THINK I'M GOING TO BE SHOCKED BY WHAT I READ IN A NOVEL?
OK! OK! YOU REALLY ARE BRAVE! GO AHEAD. KEEP IT.

FAMILIARIZE YOURSELF WITH THE BOOKS, AS A GOOD LIBRARIAN WOULD.
AND WE'LL PUT YOU TO WORK AS SOON AS POSSIBLE.

THEY WERE ONLY A FEW BOOKS, BUT TOGETHER THEY CONTAINED THE WISDOM OF CENTURIES OF CIVILIZATION.
AN ATLAS TO SHOW WHAT THE WORLD LOOKED LIKE...
ATLAS
A GEOMETRY BOOK THAT CONTAINED MATHEMATICAL AND SCIENTIFIC ADVANCES...
читаю
читаешь
читает
читаем
Грамматика
A GRAMMAR BOOK, WHICH ENABLED LINES OF COMMUNICATION BETWEEN PEOPLE TO BE PLOTTED...
A SHORT HISTORY OF THE WORLD BY H. G. WELLS: THE HISTORY THAT REMINDED US OF WHERE WE CAME FROM, AND MIGHT HELP US TO DECIDE WHERE WE OUGHT TO BE GOING...
H.G. WELLS
Stručné Dějiny světa

A PSYCHOLOGY BOOK BY FREUD, WHICH WOULD ALLOW US TO KNOW OURSELVES BETTER...
AND THREE NOVELS, ONE IN FRENCH, ANOTHER IN RUSSIAN, AND ONE IN CZECH: STORIES THAT EXPANDED A READER'S EXPERIENCES A HUNDREDFOLD.
ONE OF THEM, THE ONE THAT WASN'T FOR CHILDREN, TITLED *THE ADVENTURES OF THE GOOD SOLDIER ŠVEJK*, WAS LIKE A TREATISE ON PASSIVE RESISTANCE AND REBELLION.

AND SO BEGAN A NEW STAGE IN DITA'S LIFE.

SHE BECAME POSSIBLY THE MOST UNUSUAL LIBRARIAN IN THE WORLD.
GEOMETRIE

SHE NOT ONLY LOOKED AFTER THE BOOKS, BUT SHE REPAIRED THEM IN SUCH A WAY...

...THAT THEY SEEMED TO COME BACK TO LIFE.
GEOMETRIE

AND SO, INCREDIBLE AS IT MAY SEEM, AUSCHWITZ ACQUIRED ITS OWN LIBRARY.

IF H. G. WELLS EVER FOUND OUT THAT HE AND SIGMUND FREUD WERE NEIGHBORS ON YOUR BOOKSHELF, HE'D BE VERY ANGRY WITH YOU.

WHAT DO YOU MEAN, OTA?
WHERE HAS THIS EVER BEEN SEEN BEFORE? A RATIONALIST LIKE WELLS AND A FANTASY SALESMAN LIKE FREUD.

I DON'T UNDERSTAND...
FREUD, A JEWISH PSYCHIATRIST, THE FATHER OF PSYCHOANALYSIS, PURSUED BY THE SS, WHO FLED TO ENGLAND IN 1938...

...AND WELLS, A SOCIALIST RATIONALIST, FREE THINKER, AND GREAT NOVELIST...
...CREATOR OF A MACHINE WITH WHICH WE COULD GO BACK IN TIME...
H.G WELLS
Stručné Dějiny Světa

...AND PREVENT HITLER FROM BEING RELEASED FROM JAIL.
ALL THAT STUFF ABOUT THE MACHINE IS INVENTED, RIGHT?

SADLY, YES, BUT NOVELS ADD WHAT'S MISSING IN LIFE.
SO, DO YOU THINK I SHOULD SEPARATE THEM?

NO, LEAVE THEM WHERE THEY ARE. MAYBE THEY CAN LEARN SOMETHING FROM EACH OTHER.
BY THE WAY...

FREUD WAS A JEW AND WELLS, A SOCIALIST... SO THESE BOOKS...
YES?

...THESE BOOKS ARE NOT ONLY CLANDESTINE, BUT FORBIDDEN.

YOU'RE A VERY BRAVE YOUNG WOMAN TO LOOK AFTER THEM.
BRAVE? ME?

PLEASE CONTINUE TO DO SUCH IMPORTANT WORK, MISS LIBRARIAN.

THANK YOU. THANKS SO MUCH, OTA.

DITA, I HAVE A SURPRISE FOR YOU. WE HAVE MORE BOOKS.

GREAT! WHERE ARE THEY? WE HAVE TO FIND A PLACE FOR THEM!

YOU'RE ASKING WHERE THEY ARE? CAN'T YOU SEE THEM?
WHAT?

DITA, OUR LIBRARY NOW ALSO CONTAINS "LIVING BOOKS."

LET ME INTRODUCE MRS. MAGDA, ALSO KNOWN AS *THE WONDERFUL ADVENTURES OF NILS HOLGERSSON.*

THE "LIVING BOOKS" BECAME ANOTHER SECRET OF THE LIBRARY OF AUSCHWITZ.

SOON, PEOPLE COULD BORROW BOTH THE PAPER BOOKS AND THE LIVING BOOKS, AND MANY PEOPLE WANTED TO LISTEN TO THEM.

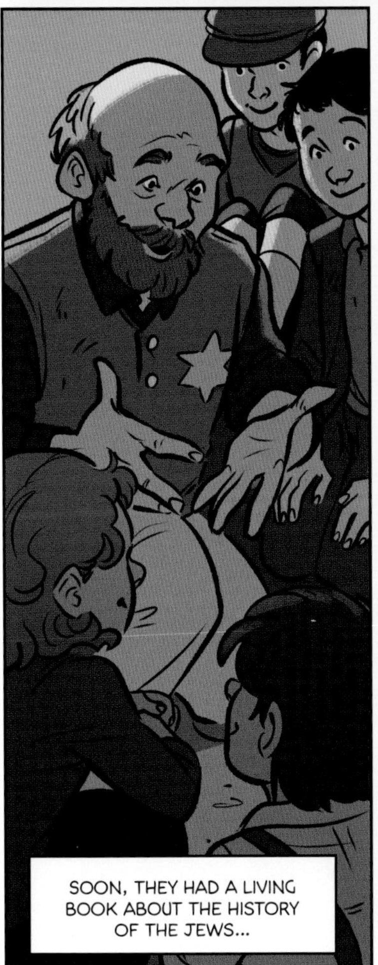
SOON, THEY HAD A LIVING BOOK ABOUT THE HISTORY OF THE JEWS...

...A COLLECTION OF STORIES ABOUT THE AMERICAN WILD WEST...

...AND MRS. MARKÉTA BECAME *THE COUNT OF MONTE CRISTO.*

DITA KEPT BUSY ORGANIZING OTHER ASPECTS OF THE LIBRARY.
PAPER BOOKS WOULD BE LENT OUT IN THE MORNING...

...AND LIVING BOOKS WOULD BE "READ" IN THE AFTERNOON, WHEN THINGS WERE MORE RELAXED.

NATURALLY, THERE WAS ALSO TIME FOR HERSELF.

DITA KEPT SOME TIME FREE AT THE END OF THE DAY TO READ.

READING ALLOWED HER TO BELIEVE FOR A FEW MOMENTS THAT SHE WASN'T IN AUSCHWITZ.

BUT THERE WAS NO QUESTION...

...THAT DITA WAS IN AUSCHWITZ...

...AND IN AUSCHWITZ YOU COULD DIE AT ANY TIME.

INSPECTION! ON YOUR TOES!

THE SS ARE COMING! INSPECTION!

QUICK! EVERYONE FOLLOW THE PROTOCOL!

WE'RE DONE FOR! IT'S "THE PRIEST," AND HE'S NOT ALONE!
THE BOOKS! IF THEY FIND THE BOOKS, THEY'LL KILL US ALL!

DITA, CHILD. WHERE ARE YOU GOING? KEEP STILL!
WHAT ARE YOU THINKING? WHAT ARE YOU DOING?
YOU'RE GOING TO GET US ALL KILLED.
ACHTUNG! NOBODY MOVE!

THEY ALL KNEW THEY COULD DIE RIGHT THEN...

...NOT JUST BECAUSE OF THE SOLDIERS OR THEIR SERGEANT...

...BUT BECAUSE DEATH HIMSELF HAD ENTERED THE ROOM.

THE ANGEL OF DEATH:
DR. JOSEF MENGELE.

FAMOUS FOR HIS CRUEL EXPERIMENTS ON PRISONERS, ESPECIALLY ON CHILDREN.

I'LL TAKE THOSE TWO.
NO, PLEASE, NOT MY CHILDREN!

SILENCE, JEWISH WHORE!

ARGH! YOU FILTHY JEW!
BE CAREFUL!
FORGIVE ME! I DIDN'T MEAN TO BE A NUISANCE.

FORGIVE ME, AGAIN! IT WASN'T MY INTENTION...

SHUT UP OR I'LL PUT A BULLET IN YOUR HEAD!

SERGEANT, CAN WE HELP YOU WITH ANYTHING?

HIRSCH, YOU KNOW THAT ONE DAY WE'LL FIND SOMETHING, AND THAT DAY...
LET'S GO! EVERYBODY OUT!

I SAID OUT! INSPECTION OVER!

THIS TIME, THEY COULD ALL BREATHE EASY.

DITA HAD SAVED THEIR LIVES WITH HER SPEED.

BUT THEY ALL KNEW THEY COULD NEVER RELAX COMPLETELY.

BECAUSE IN AUSCHWITZ, DEATH WAS NEVER FAR AWAY.

I NEVER FORGET A FACE.

I'M GOING TO KEEP MY EYE ON YOU. I'LL BE WATCHING YOU, EVEN WHEN YOU CAN'T SEE ME.

WHEN YOU THINK I CAN'T HEAR YOU, I'LL BE LISTENING.

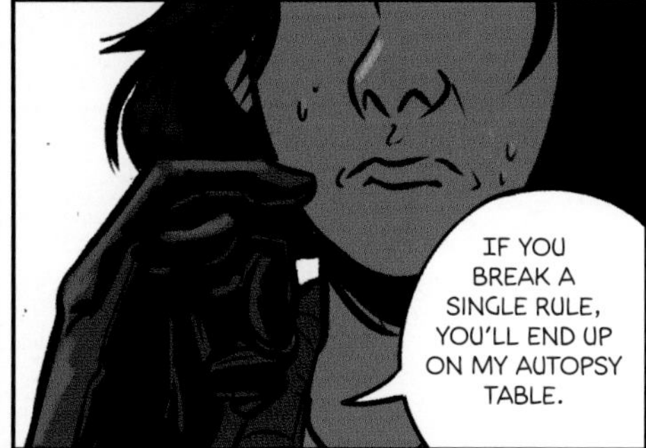
IF YOU BREAK A SINGLE RULE, YOU'LL END UP ON MY AUTOPSY TABLE.

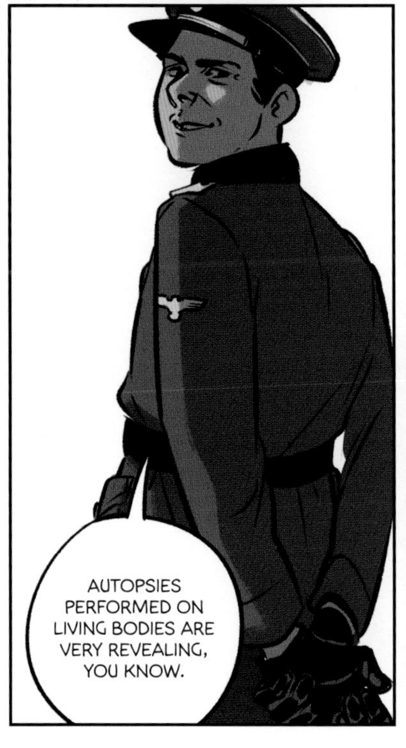
AUTOPSIES PERFORMED ON LIVING BODIES ARE VERY REVEALING, YOU KNOW.

THEY ARE AN EXTRAORDINARY SPECTACLE.

FREDY, I REALLY AM SORRY FOR BREAKING INSPECTION PROTOCOL.
DON'T WORRY. A GOOD SOLDIER DOESN'T NEED TO BE GIVEN ORDERS.

AND MY ENCOUNTER WITH MENGELE? HE SAID SUCH TERRIBLE THINGS AND...

DITA, I CAN'T LIE TO YOU. WE ARE ALL IN DANGER.

WE CAN DIE AT ANY TIME, ANY DAY.
THAT'S WHY WE HAVE TO LIVE WITHOUT FEAR AND FIGHT TO THE END.

THANK YOU, FREDY.
YOU KNOW, I'VE JUST HAD AN IDEA...

THEY'RE TO CARRY MEMENTOS OF MY DEAD GRAND-MOTHERS...
LOOK, CHILD, IF YOU'RE GOING TO LIE, I'D ADVISE YOU TO LEARN HOW TO DO IT PROPERLY.

RIGHT. WELL, I NEED YOU TO SEW ME SOME POCKETS INSIDE MY CLOTHES TO...

I DON'T WANT TO KNOW WHAT THEY'RE FOR. I HOPE IT'S FOR A GUN.
IT'LL COST YOU HALF A RATION OF BREAD.

NO, IT'S NOT FOR A GUN.
THANK YOU. I'LL GET YOU THE HALF RATION.
AND I'D ADVISE YOU TO LEARN TO NEGOTIATE. THE GIRLS OF TODAY...
DITA! DITA!

LISTEN! YOU HAVE TO HEAR... YOU HAVE TO HEAR THIS!

I'VE HEARD THAT FREDY HAS A SECRET...
...THAT HE'S A TRAITOR!
WHAT? WHAT ARE YOU SAYING? THAT CAN'T BE. IT'S A LIE.

HE'S PLOTTING SOMETHING WITH A GERMAN KAPO!
WAIT A MINUTE... THEY MIGHT HEAR US.

YOU SEEM WORRIED, FREDY.

I THINK THEY SUSPECT SOMETHING...

NO ONE
CAN FIND OUT
OR I'LL BE
FINISHED.

COME ON,
WHAT CAN
THEY DO TO
YOU...SHOOT
YOU?
IF THEY
FIND OUT HOW
I'M DECEIVING
THEM...

DITA,
WHAT ARE
YOU DOING
HERE?
OH, UM...
NOTHING!
PICKING UP A
BOOK I
DROPPED...

BE MORE
CAREFUL, DITA.
YOU COULD HURT
YOURSELF.

SHE MUST HAVE
MISUNDERSTOOD.
BUT SHE COULDN'T GET RID
OF THE DOUBT IN HER MIND.

MAYBE IT WAS TIME TO ASK SOMEONE.

WHAT ARE YOU DOING, PROFESSOR?

I HAVE TO ASK YOU SOMETHING... HAVE YOU KNOWN FREDY LONG?
WELL, WE ARRIVED ON THE SAME TRAIN.
AND WHAT DO YOU THINK OF HIM?
A VERY DISTINGUISHED YOUNG MAN, DON'T YOU AGREE?

WELL, WHAT I MEAN IS...DO YOU THINK FREDY IS HIDING SOMETHING?
OF COURSE!
WHAT?
BOOKS!

I ALREADY KNOW THAT!
WELL, YOU'RE ASKING SOME VERY STRANGE QUESTIONS.

WHAT I WANT TO ASK YOU IS IF WE CAN TRUST HIM.
I DON'T UNDERSTAND YOU, YOUNG LADY.
IF YOU THINK HE REALLY IS WHO HE SEEMS TO BE!

NO, HE ISN'T.
HE ISN'T WHO HE APPEARS TO BE?
NO, NOR AM I. NOR ARE YOU.

THAT'S WHY OUR THOUGHTS AREN'T VOICED. SO THAT THEY BELONG ONLY TO US.
SO HOW DO YOU KNOW WHOM TO TRUST HERE?

I ONLY TRUST MY BEST FRIEND.
AND WHO'S YOUR BEST FRIEND, PROFESSOR?

ME. I CAN ONLY TRUST MYSELF, DITA.
BUT DITA WOULD SOON HAVE OTHER WORRIES...

THAT DAY, THE MUCH-FEARED ADOLF EICHMANN, THE MAN IN CHARGE OF THE JEWISH DEPARTMENT, ARRIVED...
...WITH DIETER NEUHAUS OF THE GERMAN RED CROSS.

THAT DAY, THE INHABITANTS OF CAMP BIIB MADE A TERRIBLE DISCOVERY.
THERE WAS NO QUESTION THEIR LUCK WAS ABOUT TO CHANGE.

THAT DAY, THEY UNDERSTOOD THAT CAMP BIIB WAS A FAÇADE, A THEATER WITH ONLY ONE PURPOSE...

...TO PRETEND THAT AUSCHWITZ WAS A PLACE WHERE HUMAN RIGHTS WERE RESPECTED AND FAMILIES COULD LIVE TOGETHER.

THE RED CROSS INSPECTORS ONLY VISITED BLOCK 31.

THE MASQUERADE HAD SERVED ITS PURPOSE.
IT WAS QUITE POSSIBLE THAT SOON THE NAZIS WOULD NO LONGER NEED CAMP BIIB.
THAT DAY, DITA AND SO MANY OTHERS UNDERSTOOD SO MANY THINGS.
WHY THEIR HEADS HADN'T BEEN SHAVED; WHY FAMILIES WERE STILL TOGETHER; WHY THEY WERE STILL WEARING THEIR OWN CLOTHES.
PERHAPS THEIR MISTAKE HAD BEEN TO MAINTAIN HOPE.
THAT WAS THE BIGGEST MISTAKE YOU COULD MAKE IN AUSCHWITZ.
SOMETHING WAS GOING TO HAPPEN. DITA WAS SURE OF IT. BUT WHAT? WHEN?

THIS IS GOING TO BE THE LAST TIME, LUDWIG.
WHY?

I CAN'T CONTINUE TO DECEIVE MY OWN PEOPLE.
I'M NOT WHAT THEY THINK I AM.
AND WHAT IS THIS TERRIBLE THING THAT YOU ARE?

THERE'S NOTHING MORE TO SAY.
DO YOU LACK THE COURAGE TO SAY WHAT YOU ARE?

A... HOMO-SEXUAL.
CALL IT WHAT IT IS!
THE GREAT FREDY HIRSCH IS A QUEER.
I'VE TOLD YOU...!

DITA DIDN'T KNOW MUCH ABOUT LOVE.

SHE BARELY KNEW ANYTHING ABOUT RELATIONSHIPS BETWEEN MEN AND WOMEN.

AND NOW, FOR THE FIRST TIME IN HER LIFE, SHE'D SEEN TWO MEN KISS.

SHE WAS FULL OF CONFLICTING FEELINGS TOWARD FREDY HIRSCH, PITY AND DISGUST.

"HER" FREDY HIRSCH.

THAT'S WHY, A FEW DAYS LATER, DITA BEING DITA, SHE PUT HIM TO THE TEST.
YOU WANTED TO SEE ME, DITA. ABOUT WHAT?

YOU NEED TO KNOW THIS, FREDY. DR. MENGELE...
...TOLD ME HE WAS GOING TO KEEP A CLOSE WATCH ON ME.
MENGELE WATCHES EVERYONE.

ARE YOU GOING TO REMOVE ME FROM MY POSITION AS LIBRARIAN?

DO YOU WANT TO GIVE IT UP?

NO WAY!

THEN YOU'LL STAY IN YOUR POSITION.
I DON'T UNDERSTAND... WHAT ABOUT MENGELE?

WE'RE SOLDIERS, DITA. AND IT'S A LIE THAT WE'RE THE REAR GUARD.
THIS IS OUR FRONT LINE, AND WE'LL FIGHT TO THE END.

BE CAREFUL WITH MENGELE, BUT THERE'S NOT MUCH MORE YOU CAN DO.
IGNORE HIM, AVOID HIM; MAYBE THAT WAY YOU'LL GET HIM TO FORGET ABOUT YOU.
FREDY... THANK YOU.

I'M ASKING YOU TO RISK YOUR LIFE, AND ***YOU'RE*** THANKING ***ME***?
WELL...

I JUST WANTED TO THANK YOU... FOR TRUSTING ME.

THERE'S NO NEED, DITA. YOU'VE MORE THAN GAINED MY CONFIDENCE.
BUT DITA WOULD SOON HAVE OTHER THINGS TO THINK ABOUT.

WHAT? NO! IT CAN'T BE TRUE!
YES, THEY SAY HE HAS A FEVER AND THAT HE'S VERY ILL.
NOT PAPA!

YOU CAN'T GO INSIDE THE MEN'S HUT! THEY'LL KILL YOU!
LET GO! I HAVE TO SEE HIM!

DITA!
I KNOW WHAT I'M DOING!

HEY, BOYS! LEND ME TWO JACKETS. I NEED THEM!
HA HA! I NEED TWO JACKETS, SHE SAYS!
JUST LIKE THAT! WHAT WILL YOU GIVE US IN RETURN?

WHAT DO YOU WANT IN RETURN? TELL ME!
A RATION OF BREAD...
...AND LET US TOUCH YOUR TITS!

IS THIS WHAT YOU WANT, YOU PIG? COME ON, TOUCH THEM!
WHAT ARE YOU WAITING FOR, YOU SCUM?
UH...

WELL... THE BIT ABOUT THE TITS WAS A JOKE... I'M SORRY.
HA HA HA HA HA HA HA HA
THEN GIVE ME YOUR JACKET!
AND THE CAP AS WELL!

BUT, DITA...
ARE YOU SURE THAT...?
PAPA IS ILL! WE HAVE TO SEE HIM!
BUT WHAT IF THEY DISCOVER US...?

PAPA, PAPA!
WHERE ARE YOU?

DITA... YOU'VE BOTH COME?
PAPA!

YES, IT'S ME, YOUR DITA.
DARLING! I...I'M SORRY... I CAN'T...
SHH, THERE'S NO NEED FOR YOU TO SPEAK.

DO YOU REMEMBER, PAPA?

I REMEMBER REALLY WELL...
YOU LOVED US SO MUCH IN PRAGUE...
YOU LOOKED AFTER US SO WELL IN THE TEREZÍN GHETTO... I'VE ALWAYS FELT SO PROUD OF YOU, PAPA!
THANK YOU!

BE STRONG, PAPA...

THE NEXT DAY...
I'M SORRY... YOUR FATHER DIED LAST NIGHT.
NO! IT'S A LIE! WE WANT TO SEE HIM!
OH, DITA...

THEY... THEY'VE ALREADY TAKEN HIM AWAY.
THE CART THAT PICKS UP THE BODIES COMES AT FIRST LIGHT.

SOMEONE TRIED TO CONSOLE DITA...
...BY TELLING HER THAT HER FATHER DIDN'T SUFFER.

"DIDN'T SUFFER?" SHE REPLIED.
"DIDN'T THEY TAKE AWAY HIS WORK, HIS HOME, HIS DIGNITY, HIS HEALTH?

"ISN'T THAT ENOUGH SUFFERING?"
DITA...

I WAS LOOKING FOR YOU, YOU KNOW.
I'VE GOT SOMETHING FOR YOU.

YOU CAN IMAGINE HOW DIFFICULT IT'S BEEN TO GET SOMETHING LIKE THIS.

TA-DA!

I THOUGHT THEY'D BE USEFUL FOR MENDING YOUR BOOKS.

BECAUSE, AS OUR LIBRARIAN, YOU HAVE A RESPONSIBILITY.
THE BOOKS NEED YOU.
WE READERS NEED YOU.

YOU SEE, WE NEED YOUR HELP. THIS RUSSIAN GRAMMAR BOOK IS TORN...

...AND THESE VOLUMES NEED TO BE GLUED.

THE H. G. WELLS BOOK HAS DOG-EARED PAGES.

WHAT WOULD BECOME OF OUR LIBRARY WITHOUT YOU?

WHAT WOULD BECOME OF ALL OF US WITHOUT YOU?

WHAT WOULD BECOME OF...
THANK YOU.
THANK YOU, FREDY.
THERE'S NO NEED, DITA.
THANK *YOU*.

BUT, A FEW DAYS LATER, EVERYTHING WOULD CHANGE AGAIN.
WHERE DID FREDY PUT THE GLUE?

WHAT? A TRANSFER?

YES, DITA DEAR...

THEY ARE INDEED TRANSFERRING SOME OF US.
BUT TO WHERE?

WHERE? WHO KNOWS.
WHY? THAT I DO KNOW. TO KEEP US WORKING.

WORKING? ARE YOU SURE THAT...

NOTHING IS CERTAIN, DITA.

THE CHILDREN'S BLOCK...THE LIBRARY.
THEY THINK WE'RE DEFEATED...BUT WE'LL CONTINUE TO FIGHT.

DITA, I MAY NOT ALWAYS BE HERE TO HELP YOU ALL.
FREDY...

BUT I WANT YOU TO PROMISE ME THAT YOU'LL NEVER GIVE UP.
NEVER!

DITA WOULD SOON HAVE TO SHOW THAT SHE WAS GOING TO KEEP HER PROMISE.

IT HAD BEEN SIX MONTHS SINCE THE ARRIVAL OF THE FIRST TRAINLOAD OF FAMILIES.

ALMOST FOUR THOUSAND PEOPLE WERE GOING TO ANOTHER CAMP.

BUT NOBODY KNEW WHAT WAS REALLY GOING TO HAPPEN TO THEM.

AND SO MANY FRIENDS WOULD
NO LONGER BE WITH THEM...

THEY SAY THEY'RE GOING TO TRANSFER THEM TO A CAMP NEAR WARSAW.
THEY WOULDN'T DARE KILL SO MANY CHILDREN...
YOU'RE WRONG. ALL THE PEOPLE IN THE TRANSFER WILL DIE TODAY.
ALL OF THEM! THEY'VE RECEIVED AN ORDER TO EXTERMINATE FOUR THOUSAND PEOPLE TONIGHT.

IT'S TIME TO REBEL!
BUT...WHO WILL LEAD US?
HIRSCH. LET FREDY HIRSCH KNOW.
HE'S HERE. FREDY, BLOW YOUR WHISTLE! WE WILL ALL FOLLOW YOU!

FREDY, TELL US WHAT TO DO! SAY SOMETHING!
NO.
WHAT ARE YOU SAYING? WHAT DO YOU MEAN, "NO"?
WHAT IF YOU'RE ALL WRONG AND THERE REALLY IS A TRANSFER? EVERYONE WOULD DIE FOR NO REASON. INCLUDING THE CHILDREN.
NO, FREDY. WE'RE DOOMED. IT'S NOW OR NEVER!
GIVE ME...GIVE ME AN HOUR TO THINK ABOUT IT.

HE'S ASKED FOR A SHORT WHILE TO THINK IT OVER.

FINE, JUST ONE HOUR.

TIME'S UP. WHERE'S FREDY?

HAS ANYONE SEEN HIM? WHERE IS HE?

HE'S HERE! ON THE FLOOR! DEAD!

FREDY IS DEAD!

LOOK AT THOSE PILLS! HE WASN'T KILLED. HE DIED BY SUICIDE!

FREDY HIRSCH HAS KILLED HIMSELF!

NO! FREDY!

WHAT'S GOING ON?
WHAT'S HAPPENED?

WHAT'S HAPPENING?
DITA... DON'T LOOK, DARLING.

LET ME... LET ME SEE.

I WANT TO SEE WHAT'S...
NO, DITA, DON'T LOOK!

NO!

FIRST, THERE'S JUST THE SOUND OF SOBS.
THEN, THE METALLIC CLANG OF TRUCK DOORS CLOSING; ENGINES RUMBLING.
AND THEN SINGING.
THE CZECH NATIONAL ANTHEM.
THE JEWISH ANTHEM, "HATIKVAH."
"THE INTERNATIONALE."
AND THEN...ONLY SILENCE.
THAT NIGHT, 3,792 PRISONERS WERE GASSED AND THEN INCINERATED IN AUSCHWITZ.

WHY, FREDY?
WHY DID YOU DIE?
DIDN'T YOU PROMISE ME THAT YOU'D KEEP ON FIGHTING?

SO, THEN, WHY DID YOU GIVE UP?

DITA BECAME OBSESSED WITH FINDING OUT WHAT HAD HAPPENED TO FREDY. HAD HE REALLY TAKEN HIS OWN LIFE?
I THINK HE KILLED HIMSELF OUT OF PRIDE.

I THINK HE FELT BETRAYED AND HE COULDN'T BEAR IT.
WHAT HE COULDN'T BEAR WAS THE CHILDREN SUFFERING.

WHAT DO YOU THINK, MRS. TURNOVSKÁ?
SOME SAY HE WAS SCARED OF BEING GASSED...

OTHERS, THAT HE WAS ADDICTED TO THE PILLS AND OVERDID IT.
AND STILL OTHERS SAY IT WAS BECAUSE THE NAZIS CAST THE EVIL EYE ON HIM.

AND SOMEONE ELSE TOLD ME IT WAS AN ACT OF REBELLION.
THAT HE KILLED HIMSELF SO THE NAZIS COULDN'T DO IT.

DITA ASKED EVERY ADULT WHO MIGHT BE ABLE TO GIVE HER AN ANSWER.
IT'S SIMPLE: HE JUST GOT SCARED.
WHAT DO YOU MEAN?

WHAT YOU'RE HEARING. HE WAS ASKED TO LEAD AN UPRISING, AND HE CHICKENED OUT.
I DON'T BELIEVE YOU!

I DON'T CARE IF YOU BELIEVE ME OR NOT. THAT'S WHAT HAPPENED.
YOU DIDN'T KNOW HIM. THAT'S OBVIOUS.

AS FREDY'S REPLACEMENTS, WE HAVE WORK TO FINISH.
YES, BUT HE'S NOT HERE ANYMORE. WHY DO YOU THINK...?

DITA, THERE ISN'T ALWAYS AN ANSWER FOR EVERYTHING.
BUT WE'RE NOT GOING TO GIVE UP, RIGHT?

NO... NO WAY.
COUNT ON ME.

"LIEUTENANT DUB LOOKED DAGGERS AT ŠVEJK, WHO'S WATCHING HIM WITH A KINDHEARTED LOOK ON HIS FACE. RED WITH RAGE, DUB YELLED AT HIM TO GET LOST."

THE NEW HEAD OF THE CHILDREN'S BLOCK GOT PERMISSION FOR THE JEWS TO BE ALLOWED TO CELEBRATE PASSOVER.
THEY IMPROVISED THE REQUIRED INGREDIENTS TO THE BEST OF THEIR ABILITY.

THE *KEARA* PLATE WITH *ZEROAH*, *BEITZAH*, *CHAROSET*, AND *KARPAS*.

THE CELEBRATION WAS SEEN AS A MIRACLE.

NOTHING LIKE IT HAD EVER BEEN SEEN IN BLOCK 31.

THEY EVEN SANG BEETHOVEN'S "ODE TO JOY."

THEY SANG LUSTILY BECAUSE EVERYONE KNEW THE WORDS.

THEY SANG UNTIL THERE WERE HUNDREDS OF VOICES SINGING THROUGHOUT THE CAMP.

THEY SANG SO LOUDLY THAT THE MUSIC REACHED THE EARS OF A NOTABLE MUSIC LOVER.

A PRIVILEGED SPECTATOR ENTERED BLOCK 31:
MENGELE.

BUT THEY STILL SANG LOUDLY, AS IF THEY HAD NOTHING TO FEAR.

THAT NIGHT, DITA WAS PREOCCUPIED, PERHAPS STILL THINKING ABOUT FREDY.

HEY! WHY DON'T YOU WATCH WHERE YOU'RE GOING?

I... EXCUSE ME... I JUST WANTED...

I JUST WANTED TO SPEAK WITH...

...WITH THE MAN OVER THERE BESIDE THE FIRE.

I JUST WANTED...

ONLY THEN DID DITA REALIZE SOMETHING.

HE HAS FORGOTTEN...
HE'S FORGOTTEN ALL ABOUT ME.

AT LEAST SHE'D GOTTEN RID OF THE WEIGHT OF THAT SHADOW...
...BUT SHE WAS STILL AT RISK OF DYING.
SHE WAS STILL IN AUSCHWITZ...
...ALTHOUGH NOT FOR MUCH LONGER.

ALLIED PLANES HAD BEEN FLYING OVER AUSCHWITZ AND BEYOND FOR SOME TIME.
THE END OF THE WAR WAS CLOSE.

IT'S CLEAR THAT THE GERMANS ARE GOING TO LOSE.
BUT THAT'S NOT NECESSARILY GOOD FOR US.
WHO KNOWS WHAT THEY COULD DO TO US.

THE CAMP WILL BE SHUT DOWN IMMEDIATELY TODAY.
CAMP BIIB IS BEING CLOSED AND A NUMBER OF PRISONERS...
...WILL BE TRANSFERRED TO ANOTHER CAMP.
THAT CAN ONLY MEAN THAT WE'RE GOING TO DIE.
MAYBE IT'S TRUE THAT THEY'RE TAKING US TO ANOTHER CAMP.
DON'T BE SO TRUSTING. NO ONE KNOWS ANYTHING.

DITA FELT THERE WAS SOMETHING SHE HAD TO DO BEFORE SHE LEFT.

THEY WERE JUST A HANDFUL OF OLD BOOKS.

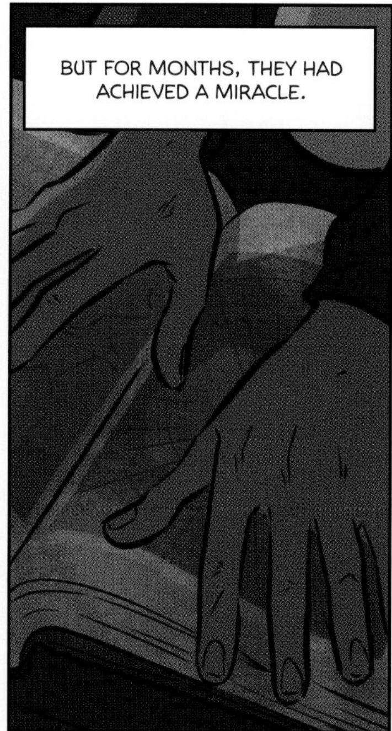

BUT FOR MONTHS, THEY HAD ACHIEVED A MIRACLE.

BY MAKING HUNDREDS OF CHILDREN FORGET THEY WERE IN AUSCHWITZ.

AND SO DITA SAID GOODBYE TO THEM FOREVER.

AND THEN, THE MUCH-FEARED SELECTION DAY ARRIVED.

SOME WOULD BE SELECTED AS SUITABLE FOR LABOR.
OTHERS, KILLED.
BUT THAT DAY, SOMETHING ELSE HAPPENED THAT WAS IMPORTANT TO DITA.
DON'T TURN AROUND.
ARE YOU THE ONE WHO'S BEEN ASKING ABOUT FREDY?
YES...
I JUST WANT YOU TO KNOW THAT HE DIDN'T DIE BY SUICIDE.

BUT, THEN, WHY... ?
IT'S ENOUGH THAT YOU KNOW THIS. GOODBYE.
THAT INFORMATION GAVE DITA SO MUCH STRENGTH.
THE STRENGTH SHE NEEDED TO FACE THE MOST TERRIFYING MOMENT OF HER TIME IN AUSCHWITZ.
NEXT!

NAME, NUMBER, AGE, AND PROFESSION.
EDITA ADLEROVÁ, 73305SB6, 16 YEARS...
...LIBRARIAN.

GROUP ON THE RIGHT, MISS "LIBRARIAN."

BY SOME STRANGE MIRACLE...

...DITA AND HER MOTHER WERE BOTH SAVED...

...BUT THEIR ODYSSEY–AND ITS RISKS–WERE NOT OVER YET.

THEY WERE LOADED UP LIKE LIVESTOCK, HEADED FOR HAMBURG.

THERE, THEY SPENT HELLISH MONTHS IN A BRICK FACTORY.
DITA'S MOTHER WAS LOSING HER STRENGTH.

THEN, THEY WERE FORCED TO REPAIR DEFECTIVE BOMBS.

NEXT DESTINATION: BERGEN-BELSEN.

THEY TREAT US LIKE CATTLE ON THE WAY TO THE ABATTOIR.
IF ONLY! AT LEAST THEY FEED CATTLE.

THERE WERE RUMORS ABOUT BERGEN-BELSEN.
THEY SAID IT WAS A LABOR CAMP—WHERE NO ONE WORKED.

MY NAME IS VOLKENRATH...
...AND IN MY CAMP, ANY OFFENSE IS PUNISHED WITH DEATH.

THEY DIDN'T WORK; THEY JUST WAITED TO DIE.

THERE WAS INSUFFICIENT FOOD AND NO WORK...
...AND NO ACTIVITIES TO CLING TO.

ANXIETY AND DISTRESS CAUSED MINDS TO UNRAVEL.

EVEN WITHOUT GAS CHAMBERS, BERGEN-BELSEN WAS A KILLING MACHINE.
EVERY DAY, PRISONERS DIED OF HUNGER, THIRST, ILLNESS.

EVERY DAY, PRISONERS WERE SELECTED TO CARRY AWAY THE DEAD.
THOSE ASSIGNED TODAY ARE...

...ADLEROVÁ, EDITA.

LET'S HOPE IT'S NOT TYPHUS OR WE'LL ALL DIE.

THEY HAD TO CARRY THE BODIES TO A COMMUNAL PIT.

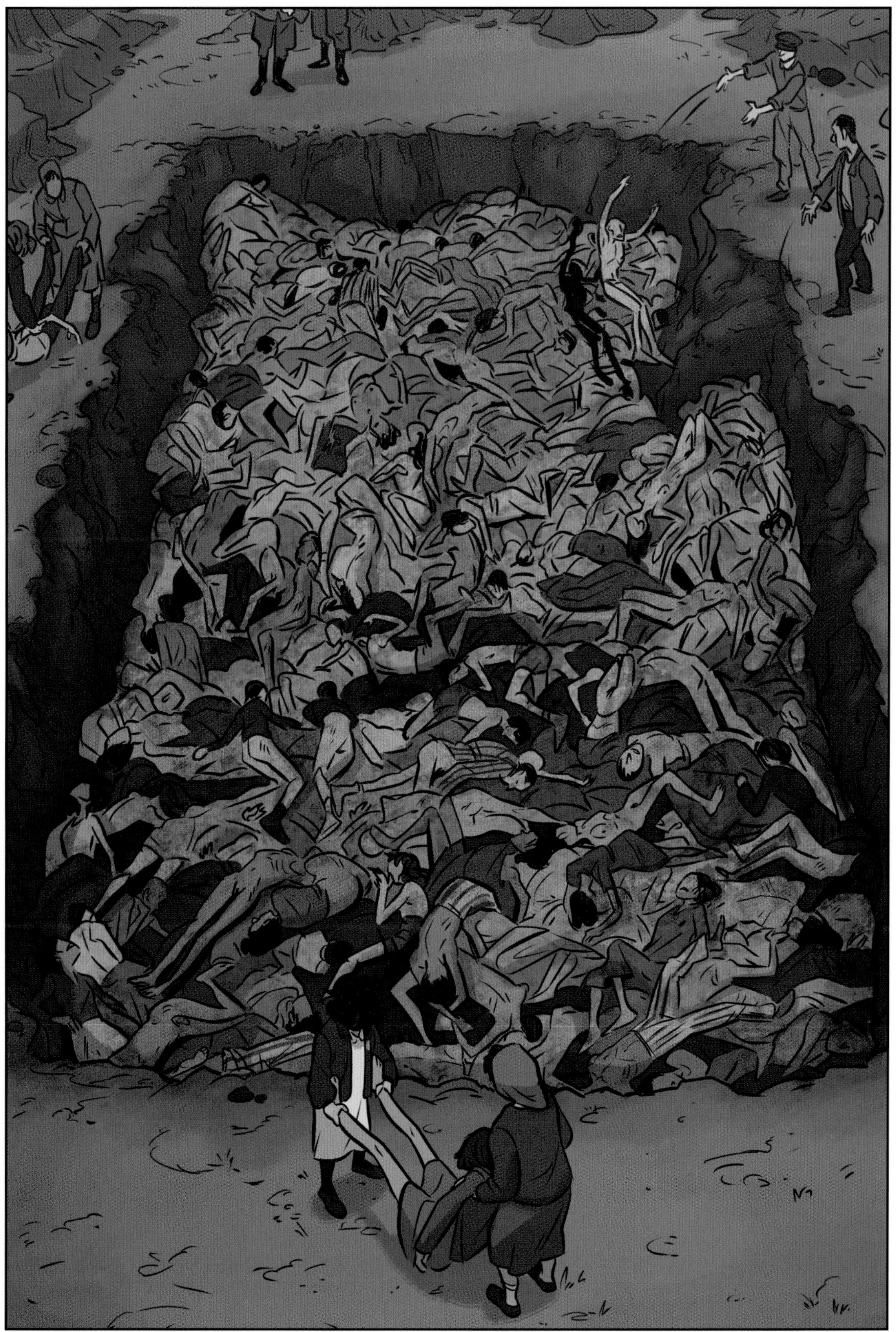

ONE DAY, SOMETHING HAPPENED.
TODAY'S CARRIERS...
...ADLEROVÁ, ELISABETH.

DITA KNEW THAT IF HER MOTHER DID THIS WORK, SHE'D DIE THAT VERY DAY.

THAT'S ME!

ARE YOU MAD? TAKING THE PLACE OF ANOTHER PRISONER IS PUNISHABLE BY DEATH.
YES, MAMA, BUT YOU NEED TO REST.

BUT SOMETIMES, EVEN IN HELL, YOU FIND THE WILL TO LIVE.
DITA?

MARGIT!

I FEARED THE WORST!
OH, DITA, I'VE BEEN SO SCARED!

THEY TOOK MY MOTHER AND SISTER AWAY IN THE CONDEMNED GROUP...
...AND EVEN THEN, THEY WERE SMILING AT ME.
THEY WERE HAPPY THAT WE WERE GOING TO LIVE.

DO YOU THINK...WE'LL SURVIVE?
HOW CAN YOU BE SO SURE?
WE HAVEN'T COME THIS FAR TO LOSE HOPE NOW, RIGHT?

IT WAS OBVIOUS THAT SOMETHING WAS GOING TO HAPPEN VERY SOON.

THE NAZIS FLED AND LEFT THEM ON THEIR OWN.

BUT THAT MEANT THERE WAS NO MORE FOOD OR WATER FOR ANYONE.

NO ONE KNEW WHAT WAS GOING TO HAPPEN.

THE ONLY WAY TO ESCAPE WAS TO USE YOUR IMAGINATION, AND RESIST TO THE BITTER END.

RESIST UNTIL IT HAPPENED.
THEY'RE HERE! RUN!
COME ON! EVERYBODY OUTSIDE!

IT WAS THE BRITISH.
THEY HAD ARRIVED TO LIBERATE THE CAMP.

THIS CAMP IS LIBERATED IN THE NAME OF GREAT BRITAIN AND HER ALLIES.

YOU'RE FREE! YOU ARE FREE!

WHY ARE THEY SILENT?
WHY DON'T THEY SAY SOMETHING?

DON'T YOU UNDERSTAND? YOU'RE FREE AT LAST!

YES, THEY WERE FREE.
THEY WERE FINALLY FREE TO CRY FOR THEIR DEAD.
THEY WERE FREE TO MOURN THEIR HUSBANDS, CHILDREN, PARENTS, AUNTS, UNCLES, COUSINS, BROTHERS, AND SISTERS...
...ALL THOSE WHO HADN'T MANAGED TO MAKE IT TILL THE END.

BUT THERE WAS STILL ONE MORE TRAGEDY.

MANY CONTINUED TO BE ILL AFTER THEY WERE LIBERATED...

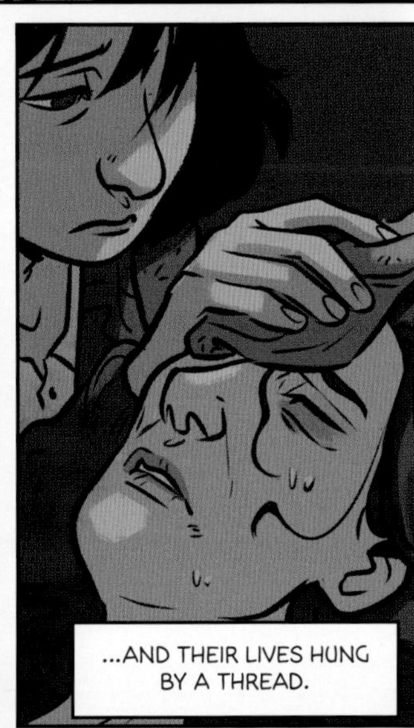
...AND THEIR LIVES HUNG BY A THREAD.

THEY'RE IN ENGLISH, BUT YOU MAY LIKE THEM.

SHE WAS ALL ALONE IN THE WORLD.

WHAT WOULD BECOME OF HER?

KNOCK!
KNOCK!
COMING!

DITA!

DEAR MARGIT...

HOW CAN I EVER THANK YOU FOR...
STOP! COME AND MEET MY FAMILY.
OR RATHER, YOUR NEW FAMILY!

MARGIT HAD STARTED A NEW LIFE IN THE SPA TOWN OF TEPLICE.

SO DITA HAD TO TRAVEL A LOT FROM THE COUNTRYSIDE TO PRAGUE AND BACK TO TEPLICE.

BUT SHE HAD A FAMILY AGAIN; PEOPLE EXPECTING HER.

SHE HAD SOMEWHERE TO START FROM SCRATCH.

THERE WERE SO MANY THINGS TO DO...

WELL! WELL! WELL! WHO'S THIS, THEN?
OUR LIBRARIAN.

OTA!
IT'S BEEN A LONG TIME, DITA.

WHAT HAVE YOU BEEN UP TO ALL THIS TIME?
WELL, I'VE FOUND WORK AS AN ACCOUNTANT.

DO YOU KNOW WHAT BECAME OF MENGELE?
THEY'RE LOOKING FOR HIM. I'M SURE THEY'LL FIND HIM.

I THINK ABOUT FREDY HIRSCH OFTEN...
HE'LL BE GREATLY MISSED.

DO YOU HAVE SOMETHING TO DO, MISS LIBRARIAN?
I HAVE TO GO TO THE JEWISH COMMUNITY OFFICE.

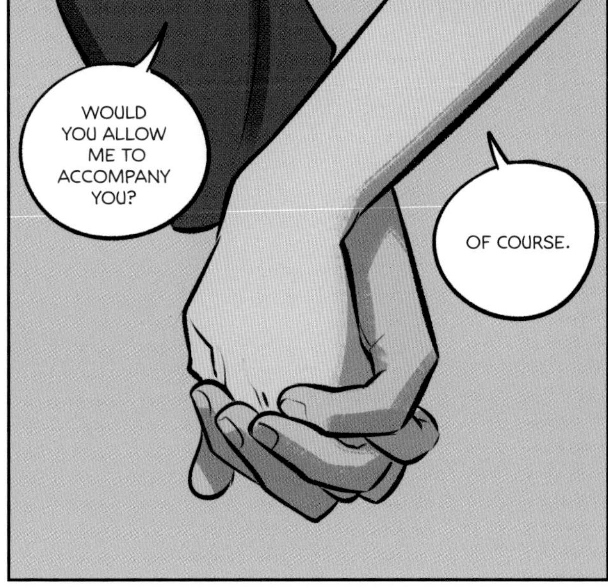
WOULD YOU ALLOW ME TO ACCOMPANY YOU?
OF COURSE.

WE HAVE ALL THE TIME IN THE WORLD FOR US...

EPILOGUE

HISTORICAL DOSSIER by Salva Rubio

From the real story to the novel that led to this graphic novel

As authors of this graphic novel, we would like to thank Antonio Iturbe for granting us the creative freedom to give visual shape to the narrative that emerges from a novel of over four hundred pages, and on which we have worked with great care to ensure that Dita's story is both recognizable to the original readers and an inspiration to new ones.

As all readers will understand, we have had to exercise a degree of artistic license: for instance, we have summarized many facts and slightly altered some parts of the storyline. In short, we've tried to create the best possible adaptation for the graphic novel environment—a format that is both visual and tells a story. To those who are interested in knowing more about Dita, her family, Fredy, Margit, and all the characters who have accompanied us for so many months, all we can do is invite you to read the original novel.

It has been our goal at all times to be faithful to the spirit of Dita's story, as told by Antonio, in the hope that this brings him many more readers. To that end, the following small historical dossier aims to provide readers with a brief context that will give them a better understanding of the events recounted in *The Librarian of Auschwitz.*

It all began when Antonio decided to take up an enormous challenge: to tell the real story of Edita Kraus (née Poláchová), who is still alive. As Antonio tells us in his book, he managed to find her in Netanya, Israel, and became friends with her. Through the writings of her husband, Ota B. Kraus, Antonio gained access to an incredible world filled by real people like Fredy Hirsch, the children of Block 31, and the surprising experiment that was the family camp (Camp BIIb), a place where death's arrival was postponed, as if it were protected by the Golem.

The Nazis and Czechoslovakia

The background to our story begins in September 1938 when Adolf Hitler, thanks to the Munich Agreement, managed to annex the territory known as Sudetenland, whose inhabitants spoke German, a fact that, to his perverse way of thinking, converted them into ethnic Germans and transformed their homeland into de facto German territory.

Hitler's real objective, however, was to eliminate the non-German Czechs (the "unGermanizable") by means of a policy of concentration camps that was implemented by the infamous Reinhard Heydrich. The non-German Czechs came to be regarded as *Untermenschen* (inferior people), like the Jews, the Poles, the Serbians, and other peoples.

This began with a plan to send the Jews to concentration camps. In some places, the first step was the establishment of ghettos—racial concentrations in urban zones. In the novel, the first step for Dita and her family was their obligatory transfer to the Terezín ghetto (Theresienstadt, in German).

Terezín: horror's antechamber

Located in the Protectorate of Bohemia and Moravia, Terezín served as a temporary place of confinement while the decision was being made as to which concentration camp to send the inhabitants. This ghetto was established in November 1941 with an initial transport of Czech Jews; soon Jews from other places arrived—Germans, Austrians, Dutch, Danish . . . But Terezín wasn't simply a staging post; more than 30,000 people died there of malnutrition and disease, and more than 88,000 were detained there.

Terezín had something in common with the future Camp BIIb in Auschwitz where Dita would be imprisoned. It was a place designed by the Germans to maintain appearances. It was governed notionally by a Jewish council, and activities such as concerts, conferences, and other educational events were permitted. But to a large extent, it was a showpiece, a front so the German Reich could demonstrate a lie to the world: that its prisoners were living dignified lives.

Auschwitz, Camp BIIb: the final destination of so many

Many of the Terezín Jews, Dita and her parents among them, were deported between September and December of 1942 to Auschwitz. Unlike the typical reception given there to prisoners—immediate execution or forced labor until it killed them—those sent to Camp BIIb experienced what might be called a privileged existence.

Indeed, those destined for Camp BIIb received somewhat special treatment: their heads were not shaved, they kept their own clothes, and they were not immediately sent to the "showers" where Zyklon B gas cut down so many lives. They were, in fact, given a curious tattoo—though the prisoners did not know its significance—with an additional code indicating they would die in six months.

The motives behind the Nazis' decision to create this exceptional little island within the deadly industry that was Auschwitz are still not entirely clear, but there does seem to be confirmation that part of the usefulness of Camp BIIb was to lie to the world: it would serve as a front should there be an outside inspection, as indeed happened, so that the Red Cross and other international bodies would believe that prisoners in Auschwitz were confined under acceptable living conditions.

Although the above description might make us think that life was better in Camp BIIb, testimonies speak of a similar brutality to the rest of the camp as far as the treatment of prisoners was concerned. In reality, according to Miroslav Kárný, the mortality rate from "natural" causes was the same as for the rest of Auschwitz, and the reasons for death were also the same: exhaustion, hunger, lack of hygiene, diseases, and hypothermia.

Camp BIIb measured 66 by 150 meters and was surrounded by electrified barbed wire. There were three service barracks or blocks, each one containing 132 latrines. The camp appears to have been close to the gas chambers and crematoriums, although these were not directly visible. There were thirty-two other barracks, of which twenty-eight were dormitories, two were infirmaries, another served as a clothing workshop, and then there was Block 31, the one we present in our story, the children's block. This was the creation of a talented man, and became a place to protect the young, at least in part, from the terrible reality that was Auschwitz.

Fredy Hirsch: a good man in Auschwitz

In the absence of a strong person like Dita as our protagonist, there is no doubt that Fredy Hirsch would be the star of this story. He was a German Jew born in 1916 in Aachen who, after a somewhat unfortunate childhood, found his vocation as a leader within Maccabi Hatzair. This was, in principle, a sporting association, but it was backed by a strongly Zionist philosophy, not unexpected in Nazi Germany, where antisemitism was official policy.

During his time with Maccabi Hatzair, Fredy stood out as a popular and charismatic leader, so much so that any prejudices an organization such as this might have had regarding his possible homosexuality were swiftly stifled. After living for a period in the regional city of Brno and then returning to Prague, Hirsch had to confront how the Germans were bearing down on the Czech Jews by removing them from their work, confiscating their property . . . He decided to create a space where Jewish children could continue to exercise, study, and take part in cultural activities.

All these initiatives proved useful when Hirsch was deported to Terezín and then Auschwitz, where he was named a supervisor in Camp BIIb, the family camp. There, using his influence with the *kapo* Arno Böhm, he succeeded in convincing the Germans to set aside Block 31 for children, using the pretext of keeping them occupied so that they would not cause problems.

Within Block 31, Hirsch made sure the children learned German, the history of Judaism, music, etc. Children's operas and plays were performed, and the walls of the barrack were decorated with drawings of characters from books. During the short period that the Camp BIIb experiment lasted, the children were able to enjoy better food and some heating, as well as strict, almost obsessive, hygiene. Thanks to these measures, child mortality in the family camp was reduced to almost zero, as opposed to 25 percent in the rest of Auschwitz. At times the SS gave in to Fredy's requests; on other occasions they punished him or interrogated him harshly.

After the visit by the Red Cross, however, the family camp lost its usefulness to the Germans. At that point, the significance of the coded date tattooed on the arms of the family camp Jews became clear, and both Hirsch and the resistance group inside the camp deduced that many of these Jews were about to be executed. As presented in the graphic novel, the circumstances surrounding Hirsch's death remain obscure: there are those who think he died by suicide, and others who think he was poisoned to prevent an uprising.

Josef Mengele: the Angel of Death

Another of the more significant characters in this story is the infamous Dr. Josef Mengele, a doctor with a degree in anthropology and a particular interest in genetics whose work had been applauded during his time at the University of Frankfurt in the 1930s. During World War II, he was declared exempt from active service after being wounded, and requested a transfer to Auschwitz.

There, he was named chief medical officer in the section for Romani prisoners, notionally to supervise other doctors. Nevertheless, he soon began to select prisoners on his own initiative, and seemed to enjoy performing terrible experiments on them, often while whistling melodies.

In his experiments, his curiosity took precedence over the pain, health, and outcomes that his treatments and interventions might have on his patients. He was especially interested in twins, eye color, and the disabled. It would require many pages to list his terrible, sadistic, and perverse experiments, and here, we can only curse his memory and all the suffering he caused.

The truth is that Mengele slipped through the fingers of the Allies because of an administrative error and an assumed name. After several years as a fugitive in various parts of Europe, he managed to escape to South America—Argentina, Paraguay, and Brazil—where he lived in obscurity, without too many problems, supporting himself by performing clandestine medical procedures, among other activities, until he died in 1979 while swimming at a beach in Brazil.

From exterminations to liberation

Meanwhile, after the arranged visit of the Red Cross to the family camp in February 1944, and after the aborted uprising during which Hirsch died, many prisoners in the camp were told they would be transferred. Those selected were driven to the gas chambers to the sound of their own singing of hymns and anthems: almost 3,800 people died that day.

At the beginning of July another selection took place, which resulted in the death of some 6,500 people. A thousand men were sent to the Sachsenhausen camp; Dita and her mother, together with some 2,000 other women, were selected for survival and worked in camps like Stutthof. Two-thirds of these women died enslaved in work camps of illnesses contracted during this period, or on death marches.

It is estimated that only 1,294 people from Camp BIIb survived the Holocaust. Dita Poláchová, the Librarian of Auschwitz, fortunately was one of them. After the war, she met up again with Ota Kraus, who had worked with Fredy in the children's block. After marrying him, she finally found much-deserved peace.

Reencounter

Storyboard and text from p. 24

PAGE 24

The following pages combine the recommendations of Professor Morgenstern with some of the scenes in the novel.

PANEL 1: Middle distance: Dita's father waving, as if saying goodbye, on the point of entering a barrack.

CAPTION: Men and women were separated

PANEL 2: Middle distance: Dita and her mother enter a women's barrack. The mother seems very frightened. Dita as well, but more surprised than anything else.

CAPTION: And each person had to find a bunk

PANEL 3: General overview: We see what the barrack looks like from the perspective of Dita and her mother: full of triple bunkbeds, full of women arguing violently.

CAPTION: Up to three people slept in a single bunk

CAPTION: There were fights for each sheet or blanket

PANEL 4: Middle distance: Dita's mother is very scared, totally out of her element. Dita doesn't seem as impacted.

MOTHER: Leave it, Dita... We'll find some place to...

DITA: Wait, Mama, I know what I'm doing.

PANEL 5: Middle distance: Dita is climbing up onto a bed, on top of it, as if she were climbing a ladder. Her mother is behind her, frightened.

MOTHER: Dita, wait, where are you going?

ABOUT THE AUTHORS

SALVA RUBIO is a writer and screenwriter, among other things. He has written graphic novels such as *Max, los años veinte*, *El fotógrafo de Mauthausen*, and *Monet, nómada de la luz*, and he works for many of the most important European publishers of graphic novels, such as Dupuis, Glénat, Le Lombard, and Delcourt. He has been nominated for a Spanish Goya award for best animated feature film. He's a member of Writers Guild of America (the union of American screenwriters) and of Spain's Academia de las Artes y las Ciencias Cinematográficas (the Academy of Motion Picture Arts and Sciences).

LORETO AROCA (Palma de Mallorca, 1994) is an illustrator and comic book artist. After finishing her undergraduate degree, she enrolled in a course in illustration at Escola Superior de Disseny (ESDi), which convinced her to pursue the goal of being an artist of graphic novels. She continued her studies in Cuenca, where she studied fine art, and in Barcelona, where she studied concept art at the Escola Joso.

In 2017, she published *Retrato de la familia Pinzón* (Ediciones SM), her first book as a children's illustrator, which was a recipient of the Luna de Aire prize. She has worked as a concept artist, focusing on the design of characters, both for Netflix (with the Art of Direction company) and with GoblinTrader. In collaboration with Salva Rubio, she has published her first graphic novel, *The Librarian of Auschwitz*, an adaptation of the book by Antonio Iturbe.